Long
Shot

Eric Zweig

James Lorimer & Company Ltd., Publishers
Toronto

James Lorimer & Company Ltd. acknowledges the support of the Ontario Arts Council. We acknowledge the support of the Government of Canada through the Book Publishing Industry Development Program (BPIDP) for our publishing activities. We acknowledge the support of the Canada Council for the Arts for our publishing program. We acknowledge the assistance of the OMDC Book Fund, an initiative of Ontario Media Development Corporation.

Cover design: Meghan Collins and Kate Moore

The Canada Council | Le Conseil des Arts
for the Arts | du Canada

ONTARIO ARTS COUNCIL
CONSEIL DES ARTS DE L'ONTARIO

Library and Archives Canada Cataloguing in Publication

Zweig, Eric, 1963-
    Long shot : how the Winnipeg Falcons won the first Olympic hockey gold / Eric Zweig.
(Recordbooks)

ISBN-13: 978-1-55028-975-6 (bound)
ISBN-13: 978-1-55028-974-9 (pbk.)

    1. Winnipeg Falcons (Hockey team)—History—Juvenile literature.
2. Hockey—Manitoba—Winnipeg—History—Juvenile literature. I. Title.
II. Series.
GV848.W55Z84 2007   j796.962097127'43   C2007-900361-3

James Lorimer & Company Ltd., Publishers
317 Adelaide Street West, Suite #1002
Toronto, ON
M5V 1P9
www.lorimer.ca

Distributed in the United States by:
Orca Book Publishers
P.O. Box 468
Custer, WA USA
98240-0468

Printed and bound in Canada

Contents

1   Hockey Night in 1896 7

2   Icelanders in Winnipeg 11

3   From the Backyard to the Big Time . . . 16

4   Struggling to a Title 23

5   Your Country Needs You 31

6   Falcons Were Meant to Fly 39

7   Same Old Problems at Home 46

8   Another League of Their Own 52

9   The Battle of Manitoba 59

10   Bigger Battles Ahead 66

11   Overseas Again 75

12   The Olympic Games 83

13   Going for the Gold 90

14   Life After the Olympics 98

15   Falcons Forever 103

     Glossary 108

     Acknowledgements 110

     About the Author 112

     Photo Credits 112

To the families of the Winnipeg Falcons,
particularly Brian Johannesson and
Frank Fredrickson, who have become my friends.
And to my wife Barbara,
who's been beside me the whole time.

1 Hockey Night in 1896

Winnipeg was hockey crazy in 1896. In fact, people all over Manitoba were in love with the game. It was a great way to stay active and warm during the province's long, cold winters.

Hockey's popularity had been growing across Canada. By 1893, even Lord Stanley, the Governor General, was a hockey nut. Lord Stanley was from England, but he decided there should be a major trophy to honour Canada's best team. So he donated the Stanley Cup to be the big prize.

At first, no league controlled the Stanley Cup the way the National Hockey League (NHL) does today. There were many small leagues around the country. The top teams from these leagues could challenge the current cup-holder. If they beat them, the cup went to a new home. Teams from Montreal won the first three Stanley Cup championships.

In 1896, the Montreal Victorias held the Stanley Cup. The champions of the Manitoba league challenged them for it. These champs were also Victorias — the Winnipeg Victorias. The two teams played a one-game series for the Stanley Cup. The game took place in Montreal on Friday, February 14, 1896. Hundreds of Winnipegers went to the station to watch their team get on the train headed east.

There were no televisions in 1896. There were no radios either. Most

HOCKEY IN MANITOBA

Hockey teams began playing in Manitoba in 1889. The following year, a small league of three teams was organized. All were from the city of Winnipeg. They were called the Winnipegs, the Victorias, and Fort Osborne. Crowds braved the cold to watch them play on outdoor rinks.

Manitobans had to wait for Saturday's newspaper to find out how their team did. But not everyone could wait that long.

Telegraph wires from the Canadian Pacific Railway (CPR) sent the story of the game to newspapers across the country. Several Winnipeg hotels had the CPR send them the reports too. The news arrived just minutes after the events took place on the ice.

"By eight o'clock," reported the *Manitoba Free Press*, "hundreds of persons had gathered in the hotels to listen to the returns." What they heard was a 2 to 0 victory for their Victorias. The Stanley Cup was coming to Winnipeg!

The Victorias returned home with their trophy on February 24. A huge crowd of people met them at the train station. When the players got off the train with the Stanley Cup, there was a parade. It ran from the CPR station to the Manitoba Hotel. Another big crowd was waiting there. At the hotel, the mayor of Winnipeg welcomed back the city's hockey heroes.

Hockey was big news all around the city. The game was catching on in many different neighbourhoods. One of the areas where hockey became most popular was in the city's small Icelandic community.

2 Icelanders in Winnipeg

People used to call Winnipeg "the Bull's Eye of the Dominion" because it is right in the middle of Canada. (Back then, the country was known as "the Dominion of Canada" because it was still part of the British Empire.) West of Winnipeg, farmers lived on the Prairies. Back east were busy cities, like Toronto, Montreal, and Halifax. People in the east needed the wheat that was grown out west. To grow the wheat, western farmers needed tools made in eastern factories. All the wheat and all the tools passed through Winnipeg on the CPR.

It took many workers to load and unload the trains. People came to Winnipeg from countries around the world to fill the jobs. The city grew quickly. Between 1900 and 1911, its population tripled. It jumped from about 40,000 people to about 130,000, making it the third largest city in Canada.

Many of Winnipeg's first citizens moved west from Ontario. Others came from England and Scotland. Some of these families made a lot of money when the city started to grow. The richest lived in mansions in the southern part of Winnipeg.

Newcomers to Winnipeg usually settled in the northern part of the city. It was called the North End. Their jobs paid very little money. Life was much harder for citizens in the North End.

Jon Fridriksson arrived from Iceland in 1890. Soon he had a job unloading freight trains in Winnipeg. Like many immigrants, he did not speak English at first. In time he changed his name to an English spelling: John Fredrickson.

John married a woman named Gudlaug Sigurdardottir. They had three children. A son named Frank was born on June 11, 1895. The Fredrickson family spoke only Icelandic in their home. Frank did not

SONS AND DAUGHTERS

Jon Fridriksson and Gudlaug Sigurdardottir were named in the traditional Icelandic way. In Iceland, children were named after their fathers. Jon's father was Fridrik Davidson. The name Fridriksson meant that Jon was Fridrik's son. The "dottir" at the end of Sigurdardottir meant that Gudlaug was her father's daughter. This Icelandic custom stopped in North America.

learn to speak English until he began school at age six.

Frank was a very good student, but school was not always fun. On the way home, children would sometimes gang up on the Icelandic kids. They were picked on because they were different. The other kids found their language and customs strange. Often there were fights.

Adult Winnipeggers also made fun of the Icelanders. They were called "Goolies." This nickname probably came from the word the Icelanders used for themselves: *Islendigur*. But the word Goolies was meant as an insult. The Icelandic neighbourhood became known as "Goolie Town." Sargent Avenue, the main street, was called "Goolie Crescent."

Icelandic parents wanted their children to have well-rounded educations. Frank took violin lessons. So did his best friend, Konnie Johannesson. Frank tried to keep off the main streets when he had his violin case. He was afraid other kids would call him a sissy. But Frank was no sissy: He was a good musician and also a great athlete. He played soccer, lacrosse, and baseball. He could walk across an entire room on his hands! For Frank, the best way of all to forget his troubles was by playing hockey.

NEW COUNTRIES, NEW GAMES

Sports and games had been important in Iceland since ancient times. North American games became popular with the people who moved to Canada and the United States.

3 From the Backyard to the Big Time

Frank put on his first pair of skates when he was five years old. He learned to play hockey on a homemade rink. His father pumped water into their backyard. With Winnipeg's cold winters, it did not take long for the water to freeze. The backyard rink was only about six metres (20 feet) long and 4.5 metres (15 feet) wide. Frank spent hours playing hockey on it.

Frank's father had not built the rink just for him. His sister, brother, and kids from all over the neighbourhood crowded onto the ice. The rink may have been the first place Frank, Konnie, and their friends Wally Byron and Bobby Benson played hockey together. Wally and Bobby were a year older than Frank. Konnie was a year younger.

A group of fathers in the Icelandic district built a small community rink. It had a shack where the boys could change into their hockey gear. There was even a wood-burning stove inside. The stove kept the boys warm in their tiny dressing room. Frank, Konnie, Wally, Bobby, and many other Icelandic boys practised their hockey skills together. They played at school and with their Lutheran church team.

The boys were barely teenagers when the Winnipeg Falcons started up around 1909. All of the Falcons were Icelandic-Canadian players. Some of the boys had older brothers on the team. For now, though, these future Falcons were still too young to play. They would also have to wait for some things to change.

Hockey had already changed from the early days of the Winnipeg Victorias. By 1909, players could be paid to play on a team. In fact, only the pros were allowed to

THE FALCONS ARE HATCHED

The Icelandic Athletic Club (IAC) formed its first hockey team in Winnipeg around the time Frank was born. It was known as the IACs. A second Icelandic team, the Vikings, was created the following year. Their games were so popular that a league was formed. The Vikings and the IACs were the only teams in it! They battled each other for a decade. In 1908, the Icelandic rivals agreed to form one team. They chose a symbol of Iceland for its name: the Winnipeg Falcons. The falcon is important to Icelanders the way the eagle is important to Americans.

play for the Stanley Cup. A lot of people thought this was wrong. They believed no one should get paid to play a game. They said that all athletes should be amateurs.

Although the pros had the Stanley Cup, amateur hockey was a lot more popular. There were only a few professional leagues, but there were dozens of amateur leagues. The top prize in amateur hockey was the Allan Cup. It was the trophy that the Winnipeg teams had their sights set on.

Only the senior, or top-level, amateur teams competed for the Allan Cup. That meant the Falcons could not play for it. In Winnipeg, the spots in the senior league were only open to the older teams: the Winnipegs, the Victorias, and the Winnipeg Varsity. Was it a coincidence that these were the English teams? The rich teams? The people who called Icelanders "Goolies?" The Falcons could not help feeling that prejudice held them back.

At first, the Falcons did play against some of Winnipeg's English teams. But they had to compete at the junior or intermediate levels. That was fine for a year or two. By the 1910–11 season, the Falcons wanted to play in the senior league. It would not be easy.

A lot of teams in Manitoba wanted to play senior hockey. There was not enough room for all of them. In fact, only one new team was allowed into the senior league in 1910–11. It was the Winnipeg Monarchs — and they deserved it. The Monarchs had been the intermediate champions two seasons in a row. It was still a letdown for the Falcons. They had tied the Monarchs for first place the year before. Besides, the younger Icelandic players — like Frank, Konnie, Wally, and Bobby — were nearly ready for intermediate hockey themselves. The older players had to move up or there would not be room for everyone to play.

The solution was to form a brand new senior hockey league. It would be separate from the old Winnipeg teams. The Falcons joined with the Kenora Thistles, the Brandon Wheat City team, and a new Winnipeg team called the AAA (which stood for Amateur Athletic Association).

The new league was a success, though the Falcons did not do very well. On the other hand, the intermediate team was starting to win. At least the future looked promising. Frank, Konnie, and the rest of the intermediate Falcons won their league championship for the 1912-13 season. Soon, the younger crop of Icelandic stars was ready for the senior team. Frank made it for the 1913-14 season.

The new hockey season was another hard one for the Falcons. They were now playing in the Independent Hockey League. The league included the Strathconas from Winnipeg and teams from the Manitoba towns of Selkirk and Portage la Prairie. The four teams played a twelve-game season. The Falcons only won four games. They lost eight. At eighteen, Frank was young for a senior player. Although his team did not do well, Frank had a very good season. He played in eleven games and scored thirteen goals.

The 1913–14 season was disappointing, but the next year would be a whole lot better. Good things would finally start happening for the Falcons.

Several players from the Falcons championship intermediate team in 1912–13 were with the senior team that won the championship in 1914–15.

4 Struggling to a Title

The start of the Independent Hockey League's new season was December 28, 1914. It was difficult to begin any earlier. Teams had to wait for it to be cold enough for water to freeze into ice. Even indoor arenas needed cold temperatures. All the arenas in Winnipeg relied on natural ice. (At that time, there were only a few arenas anywhere in the world making artificial ice.)

The Falcons started training in November. They did exercises to get in shape. The team was finally able to practise on ice on December 11. A reporter from the *Manitoba Free Press* was at the first practice. He was impressed by what he saw.

The reporter wrote about the Falcons in the next day's newspaper. "A large squad of players were out," said the story. "Judging from their speed, the Icelandic team will bear a lot of watching this winter."

The newspapers continued saying good things about the Falcons. On the day of their first game, the *Free Press* told its readers, "The Icelandic team looks like a strong one."

The Falcons' lineup had not changed much from the season before. The difference was that the older players and the younger players were more used to each other. Good teamwork was important. At the time, teams had seven players on the ice instead of six. The extra player was called a rover. Teams usually carried one or two spare players as well. They did not see much action. The starters were expected to play for all 60 minutes.

For their opening game, the Falcons had George Johannesson in goal. He was Konnie's older brother. On defense were Bobby Benson and his older brother Harvey. Frank was on left wing. Johnny Jonasson was on the right. The centre was Joe Olson. The rover was Fred "Buster" Thorsteinson. The Falcons played the Strathconas in their first game of the season. The Strathconas had been a good team the year before. But they had a lot of new players in their lineup. These players were not used to each other. They should have been easy for the Falcons to beat.

They were not.

Games at this time were played in two halves, instead of three periods like today. The first half started well. The Falcons were leading 3 to 0 after only a few minutes. But the big lead did not last long. Before the 30-minute half was up, the Strathconas scored twice. It was now 3 to 2.

The game frustrated the Falcons. They had many chances, but they could not score. At least the Strathconas were not doing much better. The Falcons managed to push their lead to 5 to 2 late in the second half. Then the real trouble started. The Strathconas scored three goals in five minutes. The game was tied. Time was almost up. Would the Falcons let an easy win slip away?

Frank came to the rescue. Just fifteen seconds after the Strathconas scored, he sped down the ice. Spotting an opening from a long way out, he fired. The shot was right on target! This time, the Falcons held on. Frank's goal gave them a 6 to 5 victory.

The Falcons only had two days off before their next game. This one was against Portage la Prairie. It was played on January 1, 1915. New Year's Day brought a new face to the Falcons. It was goalie Wally Byron. He'd been called up from the intermediate team. This was Wally's first and only game with the senior Falcons that year, but it was a good one.

The Falcons really showed their speed against Portage la Prairie. "The game was fast throughout," said the *Free Press*. "The Falcons were always dangerous, especially when they were near the goal." The game was another close one though. It took two late goals to pull out a 4 to 3 win.

With only three teams in the Independent Hockey League this year, each team only played eight games. Almost all of the Falcons' games were as close as the first two. Then, they finally took off.

On February 8, 1915, the Falcons beat the Strathconas 14 to 3. The game was every bit as lopsided as the score. The newspapers said that the Strathconas never had a chance. Reporters were as impressed by the Falcons' teamwork as by the score. "A feature of the game," the *Free Press* said, "was the fact that the 14 goals were distributed among the whole Falcon team. Everyone but Johannesson the goalie contributed to the count."

One week later, the Falcons played their final game of the season. This one was against Portage la Prairie. The Falcons beat the Strathconas all four times they played them. Portage gave them a lot more trouble. After their first win, the Falcons had lost their next two games against Portage. This game would decide everything. If the Falcons won, they would be champions of the Independent Hockey League. A crowd of nearly 2,000 people showed up at the arena that night. It was the biggest crowd the Falcons had ever seen.

The game started at a very fast pace. Play raced from end to end. Portage got the first goal. Then the Falcons evened it up. Portage scored again. It stayed 2 to 1 for Portage until near the end of the first half. Then Frank got the puck deep in the Falcons' end. He sped up the ice with it, but there were too many Portage players in his way. He fired a long shot on goal. Score!

The teams were tied 2 to 2 at halftime. The players burst over the boards after intermission. Buster put the Falcons on top early in the second half. He rushed the whole length of the ice to score a beautiful goal. Later, the Falcons stretched their lead to 4 to 2. Portage got another goal with a few minutes remaining, but they could not beat George in goal again. The game ended 4 to 3.

The Falcons were champions!

Their victory even gave them a chance to play against one of their city's top

English teams. Unfortunately, they were beaten by the Winnipeg Monarchs. The Falcons were still proud of their season, but this was not the best time for a celebration.

HOCKEY'S BEGINNINGS

Though the first Olympic hockey games did not take place until 1920, the sport has been around for much longer. Sports historians argue about hockey's beginnings. People played games with balls and sticks in Ancient Egypt and Ancient Greece. Of course, they didn't play on ice! In the early 1800s, a version of hockey was played on frozen lakes and rivers in Nova Scotia. In the 1850s, the game was played on the harbour in Kingston, Ontario. The first indoor hockey game took place in Montreal in 1875.

5 Your Country Needs You

The world was at war.

When the trouble started in June of 1914, no one knew what to expect. During the summer, things got much worse. After Germany attacked Belgium and France in August, England declared war on Germany. Canada was part of the British Empire. That meant when England went to war, Canada was at war too. Men from all around the world became soldiers.

When World War I started, people

thought the fighting would not last. They believed the soldiers would be home by Christmas. But the fighting dragged on and on. By 1915, millions of men had volunteered to fight. Thousands and thousands were killed. It seemed like the war would never end.

Naturally, the war changed the way people thought about hockey. It was silly to fight about who could play with who in Winnipeg when people were dying in real

Entire towns in Belgium and France were destroyed during World War I.

battles in Europe. So, in the 1915-16 season, there was only one league in Manitoba. To show support for the war effort, it was called the Winnipeg Patriotic Hockey League. One division had the Winnipeg Monarchs plus two military teams: the 61st Battalion and the Soldier All-Stars. The other division had the Victorias, the Winnipegs, and the Falcons.

This was the Falcons' first chance to play senior hockey in a league with their city's best teams. They did not waste it. Wally spent the whole season with the team. He was solid in goal. Frank led the division in scoring. He had thirteen goals in just six games. The Falcons battled the Victorias for first place, but it was hard to focus on hockey. The players knew that more was expected of them.

James T. Sutherland was the new president of the Canadian Amateur Hockey Association. He was also a captain in the Canadian army. He wanted other hockey players to join up too. Some already had, but many more were needed.

On December 30, 1915, Captain Sutherland delivered a message. "In a few short weeks," he said, "our hockey season will be over." He had some advice for players who were not sure what to do then. "In my opinion," the captain said, "there should only be one conclusion. That should be to exchange your stick for a Ross rifle and take your place in the army."

Frank was the first of the Falcons to volunteer. He enlisted with the Canadian army on February 23, 1916. The hockey season in Winnipeg ended two days later. Other Falcons were then quick to follow Frank's lead. Herbert "Hebbie" Axford was president of the team. He signed up on March 4. Konnie — still a member of the intermediate team — joined the army on

March 18. Bobby signed up three days later. Wally enlisted on April 1.

Joining the army meant more than exchanging hockey sticks for rifles. Wally had been working as an accountant. Bobby was a carpenter and Hebbie was a salesman. Frank and Konnie were university students. All that was given up too.

The Falcons joined the 223rd Battalion. It was an army unit made up of Canadians of Scandinavian descent. All of the men's families were from Denmark, Sweden, Norway, and Iceland. They began their military training right away. They learned to march and to use guns. They learned what it would be like to live the life of a soldier.

During the summer, the 223rd Battalion trained at Camp Hughes. It was about 132 kilometres (82 miles) west of Winnipeg. In 1916, more than 27,000 Canadian soldiers trained at the camp. In October, the 223rd Battalion moved to new quarters in

Portage la Prairie. Staying in good shape was important. Playing hockey would be perfect for that! The Falcons did not play in the Patriotic League in 1916-17, but the 223rd Battalion team did. The former Falcons fit their hockey workouts around their military training. Sometimes they used the Portage rink. Other times they practised outdoors on Crescent Lake.

That year, the Patriotic League only had three teams: the Monarchs, the Victorias, and the 223rd Battalion. All the games were in Winnipeg. That made things difficult for the soldiers. They had to take an 84-kilometre (52-mile) train ride to every game. Despite the difficulties, they gave the Victorias another hard battle.

Wally was the league's best in the nets. He allowed fewer goals than anyone else. The goalie had a lot of help from his defensemen, Konnie and Bobby. The old friends made an odd couple. Konnie was nearly six feet tall. Bobby was only five-foot-three. As usual, Frank was the scoring star. He led the league with seventeen goals in eight games played. However, the Icelandic team fell just short of the title.

Around the time the hockey season ended, the soldiers of the 223rd Battalion learned that they would soon be going to war. At four-thirty in the morning on April 23, 1917, they left Portage la Prairie on a train. They arrived in Halifax six days later. On May 3 they boarded a ship for England. It reached Liverpool late at night on May 13. Frank and Konnie brought their violins with them. To help pass the time on their long journey, they played concerts with other musicians.

The day after landing in Liverpool, the 223rd Battalion was on the move again. They took a short train ride to Shorncliffe. Troops had been training at Shorncliffe for more than 100 years. Canadian soldiers went there for more training before they were sent to fight in France or Belgium.

The day after the 223rd Battalion arrived at Shorncliffe, there was a rainstorm. It seemed as if it was always raining there. The mud at Shorncliffe was terrible. Still, everybody said the mud was much worse on the battlefields. There was really only one way to avoid the mud. That was to fly in the sky above it.

6 Falcons Were Meant to Fly

Airplanes fascinated Konnie. He saw his first one at an air show in Winnipeg in 1910. He was 13 years old at the time. Konnie had a job delivering newspapers that summer. He saved up the 15 cents it cost to see the show. He saw the planes flying, and even touched one when it was on the ground. Konnie did not have enough money to see the show again. But for the next few days, he climbed up onto a nearby bridge to watch the planes from there. He hoped that someday he would learn to fly one.

Airplanes were a pretty new invention at the start of World War I. The Wright brothers built the first "flying machine" in 1903. Just thirteen years later, the Winnipeg newspapers were filled with stories about brave pilots fighting in the air above the battlefields. That's why Konnie joined the 223rd Battalion. Once in England, he could transfer into the Royal Flying Corps (RFC). Then he would begin training to become a pilot.

The 223rd Battalion had only been in Shorncliffe for four days when Konnie, Frank, and Hebbie applied to join the RFC. Hebbie was the first to be accepted. He trained for a long time and went on to fly dozens of bombing raids with the 211 Squadron. On August 16, 1918, Hebbie led a group of bombers on a very difficult mission. They had to attack a dock in

German territory. The weather was bad for flying and there were many soldiers guarding the dock. Although Hebbie's plane was badly damaged by enemy fire, he bombed his target and made it home safely. The next day, he led another raid on the same dock. For his bravery in these attacks, Hebbie was awarded the Distinguished Flying Cross.

Frank and Konnie had very different

Konnie Johannesson looks proud after his first solo flight.

experiences from Hebbie's. After training with the Royal Flying Corps for just two weeks, they volunteered to join the battle in the Middle East. They arrived in Egypt on November 3, 1917. Surprisingly, Frank found an old copy of the *Manitoba Free Press* when they arrived at the RFC Base Depot. It made him think about hockey, and he wrote a letter to friends back home.

"Here's hoping that one of Winnipeg's hockey teams will be successful in winning the Allan Cup," Frank wrote. "I sure would like to be in Winnipeg for the hockey," he added, "but the next best place to be is in the RFC, any place."

Frank and Konnie continued their pilot training in Egypt. They both became excellent flyers. In fact, they were so good they were used to train other pilots. When Frank was sent back to England, Konnie stayed in Egypt as an instructor.

Frank left Egypt at the end of May in 1918. He was travelling on a crowded ship called the Leasowe Castle. The ship pulled out of the harbour on a beautiful moonlit night. It was carrying hundreds of soldiers and airmen. The sea was calm and the waters seemed peaceful. No one realized that trouble was lurking beneath the waves. A German submarine was on the ship's tail. It fired its torpedoes at one-thirty in the morning. The Leasowe Castle began to sink.

At first the Leasowe Castle sank slowly. There was plenty of time to lower the lifeboats. Nearby ships picked up men from the water. But some troops were trapped on the lower decks. Frank went with a group of men to rescue them. Only a few got out before there was another explosion. The Leasowe Castle began sinking quickly. Everybody who was not trapped had to get off the ship. Frank stayed so long trying to save others that he was not sure if there would be room left for him in the lifeboats. But he had one more thing he wanted to save. Frank ran to his bunk and grabbed his violin. He gave it to a captain who was already safely inside a lifeboat. He asked the captain to take good care of it for him.

Just when Frank thought all was lost, he and the few remaining men on board found a small lifeboat. They got it in the water just in time. At first the men could not move the flimsy raft in a straight line. They paddled around in circles. They had to get away from the sinking ship, or else

ARMY MEN

Bobby and Wally stayed in the army. They were sent to France where they took part in many battles on the Western Front. Fortunately, neither of them was wounded.

they might be pulled down with it. Finally, they were headed in the right direction. Just when they thought they were safe, Frank looked up. He saw a huge Japanese battleship heading straight for them.

"Oh, God," he said. "That's everything!" But the ship swerved just in time. The sailors on board the battleship dropped a ladder down to the raft. Frank and the others climbed aboard. The sailors gave them Japanese wine. They used pajamas to make bandages for the men who were wounded.

Later, Frank took another ship to Italy. From there, he took a train to England, and then to Scotland. In Scotland, he became an instructor. Frank never saw action again. Sometimes he and Konnie felt guilty when they heard about people they knew who'd been killed. But they had to do the jobs they were given. In war, everybody must do their part.

7 Same Old Problems at Home

World War I finally ended on November 11, 1918. About 600,000 Canadians fought in the war. Of that number, about 60,000 died. Another 160,000 were wounded. In all, nearly nine million soldiers from around the world were killed.

Amazingly, no Falcons player was killed during World War I. None were even seriously injured. Still, everyone had friends who lost their lives. Friends like former teammate Buster Thorsteinson. All of them saw horrible things. Now they just wanted to get on with their lives.

The Falcons returned to Winnipeg in the spring of 1919. None of them had been on skates for over two years. It was a rising young star who coaxed them back onto the ice. Mike Goodman was an Icelandic hockey player. He had been too young for the army, and too young for the Falcons before the war. Mike led the Young Men's Lutheran Club to the Manitoba junior hockey championship during the 1918-19 season. He was also the provincial speed skating champion. Mike would soon win the Canadian speed skating title too.

Haldor Halderson was another budding Icelandic hockey star. Like Mike, he had been too young for the army and too young for the Falcons. Haldor stood about six-foot-two. He was tall and thin, so people called him "Slim." Slim thought the Falcons should start up again too. He and

Mike talked about it with some of the older players. They agreed to talk with Hebbie and some of the other Falcons executives. (The executives were the people who ran the team, like the president, secretary, and treasurer.)

On August 21, 1919, a tiny story appeared on the sports page of the *Manitoba Free Press*. "Falcons to Reorganize," read the mini headline. The article said that a meeting was to be held in a few days. More meetings followed. By the end of September, it was official: The Falcons were back! A new team would be organized for the 1919–20 season.

Sports fans in Winnipeg were excited to learn about the return of the Icelandic team. "The Falcons Hockey Club ... has reorganized this year with a bang," said a big story in the September 27 issue of the *Winnipeg Tribune*. "All its old players are home once more. They've been strengthened by several youngsters who developed into stars during the war years, so the Falcons are in position to place a fast team on the ice this winter."

The newspaper praised Frank, Konnie, Wally, and Bobby for their military service. It talked about how good a team they had been before the war. The story mentioned the championship they had won. The Falcons did not impress everyone, though. Now that the war was over, the old Winnipeg teams no longer wanted the Falcons in their league. The Victorias, the Monarchs, and the Winnipegs wanted to get together like in the old days. They might consider allowing the Selkirk team to join the league. They might even consider adding the team from Brandon. But they did not want to let in the Falcons.

Hebbie fought hard to get the Falcons into the league. It was a long, tough struggle. "We players watched the battle for a place in the senior league very closely," Konnie later recalled. First, the other Winnipeg teams said there would not be enough ice available at the local arenas. Then, the Falcons heard that they would not be allowed into the league because the other teams thought they were not good enough. "That hurt," said Konnie. "And it was not forgotten."

Frank heard the same things. "They said we couldn't compete with teams like the Monarchs and Winnipegs," he would later say.

It was true that some of the Falcons had been off the ice for nearly three years, but Frank did not believe that was the real reason. "We later found out why we couldn't get in the senior league," he said. "It was because their players were from well-to-do families. They wanted no part of us."

After so many years and so many

accomplishments, was prejudice still holding back the Icelanders? Whatever the reason, the other teams soon found that they could not get away from the Falcons so easily!

8 Another League of Their Own

The Falcons still had friends in hockey. The teams they had played from Brandon and Selkirk did not abandon them. They made a pact. Either all of them would join the other Winnipeg teams, or none of them would. It turned out that none of them would.

And so a second league was formed. The Manitoba Hockey League was home to Brandon Wheat City team, the Selkirk Fishermen, and the Winnipeg Falcons for the 1919-20 season. The Winnipegs, Victorias, and Monarchs played together in the Winnipeg Hockey League. At least all of the teams agreed to one important thing. At the end of the season, the champions of the two leagues would play against each other. The winner would have the chance to become the champions of Canada in the Allan Cup playoffs.

Right from the start, a common goal

THE AMATEUR TROPHY

Sir H. Montague Allan of Montreal donated the Allan Cup in 1908. At first, the Allan Cup was a challenge trophy. That meant a team had to challenge the champion. With so many amateur teams in Canada, this became difficult to arrange. A playoff system was created with games played across the country. The top team from the west played the top team from the east in the Allan Cup final.

united the Falcons. They wanted to prove that the other Winnipeg teams were wrong about them. All the Falcons' players made sure they were in top physical condition. None of them smoked cigarettes or drank alcohol during the season.

Frank was team captain in 1919-20. He played centre. His stickhandling and hard shot were as good as they were before the war — maybe even better. On Frank's wings were the two newest members of the team. Tall and skinny Slim played right wing. With his long legs, he could dash down the rink in just a few strides. Slim was also a great passer. Both he and Frank were fast, but no one was faster than Mike. The speed skating champion played left wing. By 1919, the rover position was cut from most hockey leagues, so the Falcons had just these three forwards.

Konnie and Bobby were together again on defense. Their teamwork was better than ever. They always seemed to know exactly what the other one was going to do. In fact, Konnie always seemed to know what the opposing forwards were going to do too! He used his long reach to break up their plays. Bobby had not grown any taller, but he still did not back down from anyone. People called him "The Jumping Jack" because he leaped up to check bigger opponents.

In net for the Falcons was Wally. He still had quick hands and fast feet. Like Konnie, Wally seemed to know where other players wanted to go with the puck before they shot it. His backup in net was Babe Elliott. Babe showed up for every practice. He helped the team during workouts, even though he had little chance of playing a game. The other Falcons substitutes were Chris Fridfinnson and Huck Woodman. Chris was light and shifty, while Huck liked to throw his weight around. Huck was the only member of the Falcons who was not Icelandic.

Games now had three 20-minute periods instead of two 30-minute halves. Yet, with no rover, the six players on the ice had to work harder than ever. Sometimes it was too tiring to play all 60 minutes. That meant there was plenty of work for Chris and Huck as substitutes.

The Falcons' coach for the 1919-20 season was Fred Maxwell. People called him "Steamer" because he was so fast on the ice. Steamer had been a star player with the Monarchs. He led them to the Allan Cup in 1915. Now he was lending his expertise to the Falcons. Steamer was a good coach with a lot of new ideas. He was not bothered when his players got angry with him so long as it helped them play better.

"Hey, good looking," he would holler at

Slim when he thought the forward could be playing harder. "Go out there and get your hair messed up!"

Steamer did not just pick on the newcomers. When he thought Frank was getting carried away with a long pep talk in the dressing room, Steamer said, "Hey, Education. Save your wind for the game!"

The new hockey season was ten games long. The Falcons would play Brandon and Selkirk five times each. The key games

The Allan Cup

were the ones against Selkirk. They won the championship the year before. The team even had players who had won the Allan Cup. Joe Simpson was one of those players. He was the Fishermen's biggest star. Simpson had not won the Allan Cup for Selkirk though. He had won it back in 1916 while playing for the Winnipeg 61st Battalion team. Simpson had been wounded twice during the war, but he had survived. Now he wanted to help his home team win the Allan Cup.

Selkirk even had an Icelandic player in its lineup. His name was Harry Oliver, and he was good too. The Falcons knew that they had to be ready for Simpson and Oliver.

9 The Battle of Manitoba

The Falcons and the Fishermen opened the season on December 15, 1919.

No one gave the team from Winnipeg much of chance to beat Selkirk. Not even the players themselves knew what to expect. Nevertheless, they all trained hard. The Falcons were ready to go — and they had a surprise strategy in store for the Fishermen.

Although there was no rover, the Falcons kept three men on defense. Slim helped Konnie and Bobby. The strategy worked. The Selkirk players were baffled. They kept trying to skate into the three-man defense, but they could not get through. Even if Konnie, Bobby, and Slim did not stop the other team, their speed forced the Fishermen towards the boards. It was much easier for Wally to stop shots from the side. Soon, the Selkirk defensemen started jumping into the rush. They hoped that with three forwards plus one defenseman, they would be too much for the Falcons to stop. But this was just what the Falcons wanted. With only one man left back on the Selkirk defense, Frank and Mike pounced on him with blazing speed!

All game long, the Falcons stuck to their strategy. Three men stayed back. Two men rushed. This was not what Selkirk was expecting. They never got their game on track. By the time three periods were over, the final score was Falcons 7, Fishermen 2.

The Falcons' fans were thrilled. They buzzed with excitement as they left the arena. They could not wait to see their speedy heroes in action again. For the rest of the season, fans were willing to stand in line all night long so that they could buy tickets when the box office opened in the morning. Sometimes the lineup stretched for an entire city block.

The Falcons' second game of the season was against Brandon. They won it easily. The score was 8 to 0. But when they played Selkirk again on December 29, the Fishermen were ready for them. That night's game was a real thriller. Selkirk won 5 to 4. But the most exciting game of the season came one month later, on January 26, 1920. At the time, the Falcons were two points ahead of the Fishermen in a tight battle for first place. Everyone was looking forward to this matchup.

"Tonight's contest promises to be the hardest fought and most brilliant of the season," the *Manitoba Free Press* told its readers. "The players are now in their very best shape, the ice promises to be hard, and there is more at stake than at any other time this season."

Who did the newspaper think would win? It was difficult to tell.

"There has been much argument during the last couple of weeks about which team is better," the *Free Press* said. "The Selkirk team is made up of a bunch of stars. On paper, they look unbeatable. On the other hand, the Falcons have developed into a great machine."

Selkirk needed the win badly. The Fishermen came out flying. Joe Simpson whirled across the ice, speeding and spinning into the Falcons' end. He scored the first goal to put Selkirk up 1 to 0. The Fishermen kept coming with their four-man rush, but they could not score again. Slim evened things up at 1 to 1, which seemed to wake up the Falcons. Both teams sped from end to end, but no one scored another goal in the first period.

The fast pace continued in the second period. Selkirk swarmed all over the ice. The Fishermen went ahead 2 to 1 when a shot blazed past Wally. Then a lucky goal upped their lead to 3 to 1. A pass from a player behind the net bounced off a skate and slid in behind Wally. After that, the Falcons seemed to fade. Selkirk pushed its lead to 4 to 1, then 5 to 1. Finally, Chris got the Falcons back on the scoreboard. Even so, when the second period ended, it was Fishermen 5, Falcons 2.

In the Falcons' dressing room, Steamer had a few sharp words for his men. They listened quietly while trainers rubbed the players' aching muscles. When they came out for the third period, they were ready.

It was Mike's job to bottle up Simpson. He did it to perfection. He even set up Bobby for a goal that made the score 5 to 3. Then Frank set up Slim to make it 5 to 4. When Mike scored again, the Falcons' fans erupted in cheers! The score was now 5 to 5.

Both teams were exhausted as the game headed into overtime. With time running out in the extra period, Wally moved quickly to stop a hard shot from close range. Bobby grabbed the rebound and sped up the ice with the puck. He fired a hot shot at the Selkirk net, but the goalie made the save. The puck rebounded to Slim. He made a wild swing and batted it into the net!

Falcons 6, Fishermen 5.

The fans went crazy.

The Falcons were just one win away from the league title. When they beat the Fishermen 5 to 3 in their next meeting, the championship was theirs! Frank scored four goals in the clinching game. He finished the year with 23 goals in just ten games, beating out Simpson from Selkirk for the scoring title. Wally led the league with two shutouts and a goals-against average of 2.57. Bobby led the league in penalty minutes, although he only had 26.

As champions of the Manitoba Hockey League, the Falcons got what they wanted. They had a chance to show up the teams that had once again tried to keep them out of senior hockey.

OTHER FALCONS

Harvey Benson, Ed Stephenson, Connie Neil, and Babs Dunlop also played for the Falcons during the 1919-20 season. They were substitute players who each saw action in a few games. All of them could be counted on when needed.

10 Bigger Battles Ahead

The Winnipegs came out on top in the Winnipeg Hockey League. The Falcons would face them in a two-game series. The total score of both games would be added together to determine the winner. The team that won the provincial championship would advance to the semifinals of the Allan Cup playoffs.

Game one against the Winnipegs was on February 26, 1920. "The Icelanders are favorites," said the *Manitoba Free*

Press, "but the Winnipegs should make things interesting. The Falcons have developed a system that is hard to beat … but the Winnipegs cannot be treated lightly." Everyone was sure the games would be close. People were told to get their tickets early. "The rink will likely be jammed to the doors," warned the *Free Press*.

The rink was filled with 4,500 fans for game one. The Winnipegs looked good in the early going. Then, at 5:20 into the first period, Slim broke away. He sped up the ice with the puck and passed it to Frank. He blasted it into the net! After that, it was all Falcons. Frank scored four more goals, and the Falcons had a 5 to 0 victory. Wally only had to make nine saves all night. The Falcons fired 41 shots at the Winnipegs' goalie.

The total score from both games counted, so the Winnipegs had to win by at least six goals in game two. Nobody thought they could do it. Still, the Winnipegs promised to make things tough for the Falcons on March 2. It was not a promise they could keep. Frank scored six more goals. He set up Konnie for another. Slim scored two and set up Huck for the final goal. Wally had to face 19 shots this time. He just missed a second shutout. The final score was 10 to 1. The Falcons won the series 15 to 1.

The Falcons had proved they were every bit as good as the other Winnipeg teams. In fact, they were much, much better! The Allan Cup was in their sights now. If a chance to win the Canadian championship was not exciting enough, there was something even bigger at stake that year. Whichever team won the Allan Cup would represent Canada at the world's first Olympic hockey tournament.

The Olympic Games had been

cancelled in 1916 because of the war. They were to restart in 1920. The Games would take place during the summer in Antwerp, Belgium. The International Olympic Committee wanted to do something important to celebrate their return. They decided to hold a special Olympic competition in the spring. There were no Winter Olympics then, so the spring event would include some winter sports. Hockey fans were very excited about this decision. However, in later years, people would find the idea of a spring tournament with winter sports that was part of the Summer Olympics very confusing!

There was still one team to defeat before the Falcons could even think about the Allan Cup final or the Olympics. That team was the Fort William Maple Leafs. The Falcons would play another two-game series against them with the total goals to count. Whichever team won this semifinal series would be the champions of Western Canada. The winners would travel to Toronto to face the champions of Eastern Canada. Whoever won that series would take home the Allan Cup.

Fort William was a hard-checking team. They went right after the Falcons in game one of their series. At first, they seemed to have the Falcons all bottled up. But not for long! By the end of the game on March 8, the Falcons had scored seven times. The Maple Leafs only scored twice. Game two was played two nights later. The result of that matchup was even more lopsided. The Falcons won 9 to 1. They took the series 16 to 3.

On March 23, 1920, the new champions of Western Canada boarded a train for the two-day trip to Toronto. A huge crowd of fans showed up to wish the Falcons well.

The players posed for pictures. Confident smiles were on their faces.

When the Falcons arrived in Toronto, they found the city alive with excitement over the Allan Cup. The hockey team from the University of Toronto (U of T) had just won the eastern playoffs. Toronto fans had not expected a hometown team to reach the final. "Toronto has gone hockey mad," the newspapers said. Chris's cousin Bill Fridfinnson was one of the Falcons' executives. He agreed. In a letter to his girlfriend, Bill wrote, "You can't imagine how crazy this city is about hockey."

The last few tickets for the Allan Cup final went on sale at 10 o'clock in the morning on Friday, March 26. Fans started lining up for them at 10 o'clock on Thursday night. About 500 fans showed up on Friday morning just to watch the Falcons practise! The *Manitoba Free Press* said that "never in the history of hockey has there been more interest shown over a series." Toronto's Arena Gardens held over 8,000 fans. It was practically filled to the roof on Saturday night.

The Falcons skated circles around the U of T team in the first few minutes of game one. However, the first period was almost over before Frank finally scored. It was 1 to 1 after one period, but the Falcons scored four times in the second. They got three more in the third. "The Falcons simply skated the college lads dizzy," wrote Lou Marsh in the *Toronto Star*. "Everybody who saw Saturday's game will say so. The Falcons had more speed on one team than we ever saw here before."

The Falcons won the game 8 to 3. Frank had four goals. Mike had three. Huck got the other. Nobody thought the U of T players could make up the five-goal difference in game two. Marsh said that "only a miracle" could keep Toronto's hopes alive.

With hard checks, U of T managed to slow down the pace in the second game. Still, the Falcons led 2 to 1 after two periods. But early in the third, Toronto almost got its miracle. A U of T player fired a long shot on goal. Wally did not see the puck coming at him. Goalies did not wear masks in those days. The flat edge of the puck hit Wally on the left eye. He crumpled to the ice. There was blood everywhere. The puck had opened a five-inch cut above Wally's eye. There was a smaller cut below it. It took fifteen minutes to stitch his wounds. Wally was in no condition to go back in the net. Babe, the team's practice goalie, had to take over. He had not played in a game all year, but all his hard work paid off. Babe did the job and the Falcons went on to a 3 to 2 victory.

They were almost barred from playing hockey in their own city. Now they were champions of the entire country. Next, the Falcons were going to the Olympics to take on the world.

The Allan Cup ceremony

11 Overseas Again

The Falcons had little time to celebrate being champions. They won the Allan Cup on March 29. The Olympics were starting on April 20. In order to make it to Antwerp on time, the team had to set sail from Saint John, New Brunswick, on April 3. The Falcons had hoped to return to Winnipeg for a parade. That would be impossible. There was not even time to go home and get clean clothes!

Hockey fans in Toronto helped raise

money so the Falcons could buy some of the things they needed. The mayor of Toronto even wrote a letter asking local businesses to help. Winnipeg raised $500 for the team. The government of Manitoba added $2,000. Now that the

The Falcons on board their ship to Europe. Top to bottom: Konnie and Slim, Frank and Huck, Wally, Chris and Mike, Bobby.

Falcons were Canada's team, everybody wanted to help them.

The Falcons left Toronto by train on the night of April 1. They made a short visit to Montreal the next morning, and then continued on to Saint John. On April 3, they boarded a ship for the next leg of their journey. It would take them to Liverpool, England. All eight of the Falcons' regular players were on board. So were team executives Hebbie and Bill. Team trainer Gordon Sigurjonsson also made the journey. Sadly, Steamer was not able to go. The coach had a job in Winnipeg that he needed to return to right away. But Steamer had trained his men well. He knew they would get along without him. "It's sure great to be the coach of such a fine gang of athletes," he said. "I know they are capable of defeating the best amateur hockey teams in the world."

The seas were calm for the first few days of the Falcons' ocean voyage. Then the weather turned rough. The players joked about which of them might get seasick. The first one to throw up would have to pay a fine. Frank wrote about it in a letter to Bill Finlay of the *Manitoba Free Press*:

"As yet the only sick man in our crowd is Trainer Sigurjonsson. He has never yet been on a sea voyage without being sick. Slim, Mike, Bobby, Wally, Konnie, and myself have all been practising a dash for the rail. Slim says if it gets much rougher that he's going to jump off and walk to shore."

Bill sent letters home to his girlfriend. He told her that there were a lot of people from Winnipeg on the ship. "They have certainly advertised who we are," he wrote. "Everybody on board from the Captain to the stoker knows that we are the Falcons of Winnipeg." According to

Bill's letters, the Falcons were very popular with everyone on the ship — and not just because they were hockey stars on their way to the Olympics.

"Tonight we organized a dandy concert in the largest lounge room. Frank and Konnie started it with a duet on their violins. A splendid young piano player from Vancouver joined them. Soon we had 200 people or more in the room."

Frank, Konnie, and the piano player became known as The Falcon Trio. They

A FRIEND IN FINLAY

Frank was good friends with *Manitoba Free Press* sports editor Bill Finlay. It was probably no coincidence that the newspaper covered so many Falcons games! Frank later said that Finlay helped get the Falcons back into hockey after the war. He encouraged the team to start playing again.

were in demand for concerts and dances on the ship. They played high-class opera music as well as popular jazz tunes. Sometimes, Frank and Konnie would take their violins below deck to play concerts for the passengers in steerage. These were the third-class passengers — the poorest people on the ship. They were not allowed into the fancy lounges on the upper decks. The Falcons knew all about this kind of unfairness.

While they were on the ship to England, the Falcons got the new uniforms they would wear at the Olympics. Traditionally, the Falcons' colours had been black and orange. During the 1919-20 season, they wore orange sweaters with three black stripes. The word FALCONS was on the chest. For the Olympics, they were given golden yellow jerseys with black collars and cuffs. There was also a black band across the middle and a large red maple leaf. Inside the leaf, the word CANADA was written in white letters. All of Canada's Olympic athletes wore these colours in 1920.

The day after they got their Olympic jerseys, the players showed them off while they worked out. There was nowhere on

On the ice at the Olympics for Canada are Gordon Sigurjonsson, Hebbie Axford, Wally Byron, Slim Halderson, Frank Fredrickson, Bill Hewitt, Konnie Johannesson, Mike Goodman, Huck Woodman, Bobby Benson, Chris Fridfinnson, and Bill Fridfinnson.

the ship to hold a real practise, but they had to do something to stay in shape. So they jogged on the deck, played leapfrog, and skipped. Mostly, though, the Falcons passed the time by playing chess or cards. "We have played so much cards," wrote Bill, "that we are getting fed up with it."

After nine days at sea, the Falcons' ship finally arrived in Liverpool. That same day, they boarded a train to London. After two days of sightseeing, the Falcons were off again. This time, they took a train to Dover. Next came a short boat ride across the English Channel to Ostend in Belgium. Then they took another train to Antwerp. Two weeks after leaving Toronto, the Falcons arrived at the Olympics.

12 The Olympic Games

Seven countries took part in the first Olympic hockey tournament at Antwerp in 1920. Everyone knew that only two countries had a real chance to win the gold medal. One was Canada. The other was the United States. The Falcons would face the Americans in their second game at the tournament. That was not going to be their only challenge.

The style of hockey played at the Olympics would be quite different from what the Falcons were used to. For one thing, the old rule of seven-man hockey was being used. Either Huck or Chris would be in the lineup as the rover. No substitutes were allowed. All seven men would have to play the whole game. However, each game would only be 40 minutes long instead of 60. There would be two halves of 20 minutes each. Even so, the tournament was going to be tiring. The Falcons were scheduled to play three games on three straight days. At least if they won all three games, they would be done playing. They would be the champions.

Perhaps the most unusual part of the 1920 Olympic hockey tournament was the rink where it was played. The *Palais de Glace* (Ice Palace) in Antwerp was a beautiful arena, but it had not been built for hockey. The ice surface was only about 56 metres (185 feet) long and 18 metres

(59 feet) wide. Official hockey rinks in Canada and the United States were 61 metres (200 feet) long and 26 metres (85 feet) wide. Normally, the Belgian arena was used for pleasure skating. Its boards were very flimsy. There were no seats. Instead, it had tables and chairs, as well as space for an orchestra. Music was played during all of the Olympic hockey games.

The *Palais de Glace* took some getting used to, but at least the Falcons had arrived early in Antwerp. They had time for a few practices. The team could work out some plays for seven-man hockey and adjust to their strange surroundings. There was also time to scout their European opponents.

The first team the Falcons saw was from Sweden. They were not very impressive. The Swedes were dressed more like a soccer team than a hockey team. Most of them just wore small knee pads. Their shins were protected by golf socks! Not even the

Swedish goalie wore much protection. He had no chest protector and only a skinny pair of pads to protect his legs.

When the Falcons saw the Swedes play, they understood why the European team used so little equipment. Instead of powerfully shooting the puck, they just flipped it. There was very little strength behind their shots.

The goalie from Switzerland looked even more unusual than the Swedish goalie. Frank thought that he was probably the worst goalie he had ever seen. "He held his stick like a manure shovel," Frank said. The goalie did not have much padding either. Plus he was wearing a shirt and a tie!

A defenseman from France was the oddest-looking player of them all. He was much older than any other player and he wore glasses on the ice. He also had a thick, black beard that came halfway down his chest. "I wonder if he'll get a penalty if the puck gets lost in there," joked Mike.

In fairness, the Falcons looked just as funny to the European players. Some of them actually laughed when they saw the Falcons' uniforms. Why did they wear so much protective equipment? They found out soon enough. When the Falcons warmed up at their very first practice, some of their shots actually broke the boards around the rink. No one was laughing

The Swiss goalie wore a shirt and tie under his sweater. Like other European teams, none of the Swiss players wore very much protective equipment.

after that. The Europeans could not believe how fast the Falcons skated. Some people thought Mike had motors in his skates!

It was obvious to the Falcons that they were a lot better hockey players than the Europeans were. They also knew what it was like to be the underdog. So, the Canadians decided to help the other players. "It was one of the customs our boys instituted," said Bill Hewitt of the Canadian Olympic Committee. "We virtually trained the Swedes, Czecho-Slovaks, Belgians and French teams." The Falcons also decided that they would not embarrass their opponents. "We tried to limit ourselves to 14 or 15 goals against the European teams," Frank explained. "Believe me, it was difficult!"

The Falcons played their first Olympic game on April 24, 1920. The game was against Czechoslovakia. The Falcons took it easy on them. They had fun passing the puck between themselves on the way to the Czech net. The final score was 15 to 0. Slim had seven goals. Frank got four. Mike had two. Huck and Konnie scored one apiece. Wally's eye was fine now. He earned an easy shutout.

The United States also played their first game that day. They played against Switzerland. The Americans had not been together for years. They were an all-star team. The players were picked from the best American amateur clubs. As a result, they were a bunch of individual stars. They lacked the Falcons' teamwork, but they did have plenty of talent. In their first game, the United States beat Switzerland 29 to 0!

The Falcons knew the Americans would be the toughest team they had ever faced. It would be a hard fight. Whichever team won the game would be certain to win the gold medal.

13 Going for the Gold

The big game between Canada and the United States was on Sunday, April 25, 1920. It was set for nine o'clock that night. People began filling the streets outside the *Palais de Glace* at six o'clock. By 8:30, the arena was so jammed with fans that the doors had to be closed. No one else was allowed inside. The arena only held about 1,600 people. It seemed like ten times that number had tried to get tickets. It was so crowded that special squads of soldiers were needed to get the players inside safely. Men in tuxedos and top hats begged the players to let them carry something for them so they could sneak inside. Mike had about eight men following him, each one carrying a different piece of his equipment. Wally let three others help him. This was going to be the greatest hockey game ever played in Europe. Everyone wanted to see it.

The Falcons, in their golden yellow uniforms, were the first team on the ice. The orchestra played "O Canada" as the players lined up in front of the Prince of Belgium's royal box. Then the Americans came out. They wore dark blue jerseys with small U.S. flags on the chests. They lined up while the orchestra played "The Star Spangled Banner." When the music was over, it was time to play.

Frank took his position at centre. Slim was on his right. Mike was at left wing.

Huck was behind them, playing rover. Konnie and Bobby were on defense. Wally was in goal.

Frank won the opening faceoff. The Falcons sped to attack. They rushed right into the American end. The Canadian forwards buzzed in and out. They controlled the play for the first ten minutes. Frank and Slim fired shot after shot, but they could not get the puck in the net. For the rest of the first half, play was more even. When the Americans took control,

The Americans were by far the toughest team the Falcons faced at the Olympics.

Mike always sped back to help. If anyone got past Mike and Huck, Konnie and Bobby were there to stop him. When a shot did get through, Wally was in position to make the save. At the end of 20 minutes, there was no score. The big crowd was anxious for a breakthrough.

Frank was frustrated. "I had a bad first period," he said. "I think I missed more chances than I ever did before. I hit the post. I hit the crossbar. I drilled it into the side of the net. I couldn't get it in." Frank might not have been happy with his play, but the European fans were amazed by the skill of the two teams.

"I have never seen anything like this sports competition," wrote a reporter for a Swedish newspaper. "Every single player on the rink is a perfect acrobat on skates. They jump over sticks and players with ease and grace. They turn sharply with perfect ease and without losing speed.

They skate backwards just as easily as forwards.

"The small puck was moved at an extraordinary speed around the rink. The players fought for it like seagulls that flutter after bread crusts from a boat. The players attacked each other with a roughness that would have knocked you into the next week. The Canadian defender Johannesson was pushed headlong into the barrier board so hard that it was cracked. However, he happily continued to play on as if nothing had happened.

"And there were shots at goal! The players ... could send the puck towards the goal so hard that you could not follow it with your eyes. The goalkeepers had to dart about like mad ... A few times the Canadian goalkeeper had to stop the puck with his hand. Despite his thick gloves, his fingers were smashed until they bled."

After all that action, the intermission

lasted just five minutes. When play started again, it was the Americans who came out flying. Then the Canadians began to take over. About midway through the second half, Frank sped down the ice on a breakaway. He fired a hard shot, but the American goalie stopped it. When he could not control the rebound, Frank pounced. He shot again and scored!

Canada 1, United States 0.

The Americans stormed back, but they could not get a shot past Wally. Then, with about five minutes to go, Slim and Mike sped up the ice together. After a few quick passes, the puck was dropped back to Konnie who fired it in. Five minutes after that, the game was over. The Falcons won 2 to 0.

"It was anybody's game until near the finish," said the manager of the American team. "But the best team won."

Now, the only thing that stood between

Canada and hockey's first Olympic gold medal was Sweden. Even the Swedish players knew they had no chance. They were right. The Falcons beat them 12 to 1. Frank had seven goals. Slim had two. Mike, Bobby, and Chris had the rest. The biggest surprise was not the score. It was the fact that Sweden actually managed to get a goal.

"They were without a doubt the best of the European teams," Frank said. "They were very friendly fellows and we liked them a lot. I guess it's safe to say we gave it to them."

Reports of Sweden's goal are all a little different. Most say the Falcons were already winning 5 to 0 at the time. Others say it was 3 to 0. Some say the puck bounced in off somebody's leg. Others say the Canadian players all seemed to fall down when the Swedish scorer got near the net. However it happened, everyone seemed happy with the result.

"The Swedes went wild," Frank said. "They were yelling and cheering. They shook hands with themselves. They shook hands with us. It was great."

PARTING GIFTS

With no more games to play, the Falcons gave their sticks to the Swedish players. The Canadians would have gold medals to take home as Olympic souvenirs.

14 Life After the Olympics

The Winnipeg Falcons were champions of the world. Newspapers across Canada could not say enough good things about them. Reporters praised the players for their skill, but were even prouder of their sportsmanship. Big plans were made to honour the Falcons when they returned home. The Falcons were invited to two banquets while they were still in Antwerp.

The Olympic medals were handed out on April 29. Under the tournament's strange format, the three teams that lost to the Falcons played for the silver medal. The United States won it. Then Czechoslovakia upset Sweden for the bronze. After the medals were handed out, the Falcons left Antwerp to tour the battlefields of World War I. Then they were off to Paris for more parties and banquets. On May 5, the Falcons boarded a ship in Le Havre, France. It took them home to Canada. They arrived in Montreal late at night on Saturday, May 15.

The next day, the Canadian parties and banquets began. Sir H. Montague Allan, the man who donated the Allan Cup, invited the Falcons to a luncheon. Next they caught a train to Toronto. On May 17, there was a big reception for the team on the steps of Toronto's city hall.

"You are a credit to Canada," said Mayor Thomas Church. "You played a clean game and are a credit to your home city. Winnipeg is to be congratulated on having such a fine body of men."

Each player was presented with a silver-headed cane. Then they were taken to a baseball game and given a tour of Toronto's waterfront. That night, there was a banquet at the King Edward Hotel, one of the fanciest hotels in the city. Over the next two days, Mayor Church and several other important citizens gave parties in their homes for the Falcons. Finally, on the evening of May 20, the Falcons boarded the train that would return them to Winnipeg.

"All Winnipeg will turn out to give the Falcons welcome," said the *Manitoba Free Press*. "And right royally it is to be extended! They are kings in the realm of hockey. The splendid sportsmanship and great prowess of this splendid band of athletes have conferred honour and distinction not only on Winnipeg, their native city, but upon all Canada as well. Make it a hot one!"

The Falcons' train arrived in Winnipeg in the afternoon on Saturday, May 22. A half-day holiday was declared in their honour. They had been gone for almost exactly two months. Now the party would really begin!

An hour before the train pulled in at the CPR station, a siren was set off in the city. It signalled everyone to get ready for the celebration. Hundreds of family members, friends, and supporters went to the station to greet the Falcons. Mayor C.F. Gray officially welcomed the team home. Then the parade began.

Thousands of people lined the streets. Everyone in Winnipeg who owned a car was invited to decorate it with the Falcons' colours. There were cars, trucks, horse-drawn carriages, and even airplanes in the parade. It made its way out of the train station and down Main Street. Then it turned up Portage Avenue and headed for the baseball stadium at Wesley Park. The stadium held 7,000 people, so it was the perfect place for the official presentation of the Allan Cup. Later that night, there was a banquet at the Fort Garry Hotel. At the banquet, every member of the team was presented with a brand new gold pocket watch, compliments of the City of Winnipeg. Banquets were held practically every night during the following week. It was a time the players would never forget.

15 Falcons Forever

Just three years later, none of the Olympic champions were playing for the Falcons anymore. Most of them moved on to professional hockey teams. A few even made it to the National Hockey League. Konnie played pro hockey until 1929. Wally played until 1932. Mike lasted all the way until 1939. Bobby and Slim also had long careers. Both of them played a few games in the NHL. Bobby played for the Boston Bruins during the 1924–25 season.

Slim split the 1926–27 season between Detroit and Toronto.

To no one's surprise, Frank enjoyed the most success after his days with the Falcons. Frank turned pro in 1920 as a member of the Victoria Aristocrats. Victoria played in the Pacific Coast Hockey Association (PCHA), a league that used to play against NHL teams for the Stanley Cup. Frank played four seasons in the PCHA and led the league in scoring twice. Slim also played for Victoria. They were known as the Cougars by 1924–25. The team was then playing in the Western Canada Hockey League. That year, Frank and Slim helped the Cougars win the Stanley Cup. Later, Frank played four seasons in the NHL. In 1958, he was elected to the Hockey Hall of Fame.

Even as a star professional hockey player, Frank never earned more than $8,000 in a season. He and all the other ex-Falcons needed jobs outside of hockey. Wally worked for an oil company. Slim was an accountant. Bobby worked for a department store. Mike ran a laundry. Huck managed a paint company. Frank coached university hockey teams and later became a politician in Vancouver. Konnie flew airplanes. Both he and Frank trained pilots again during World War II.

Over the years, the Falcons players all got married. They raised families and grew old. People's memories of their glory days faded. Chris was the first to pass away. He was only 40 when he died in 1938. Mike was the last survivor. He was 93 years old when he died in 1991. By the time of Mike's death, there were very few people who still remembered the story of the Winnipeg Falcons.

Then, in the fall of 2001, an announcement was made. Team Canada was going to wear special sweaters at the 2002 Salt

Lake City Winter Olympics. The sweaters would have a special logo. It would honour Canada's first Olympic hockey champions. But the team they were to honour was the Toronto Granites!

It was an honest mistake. After all, the Toronto Granites had won the gold medal at the first official Olympic Winter Games in 1924. The Falcons had not been part of the Winter Olympics. People were not sure any longer which competition they had played in. Almost everyone had forgotten that the spring tournament in 1920 had been part of the Summer Olympics.

The children and the grandchildren of the Winnipeg Falcons had not forgotten. Neither had other proud Icelandic Canadians. To them, Team Canada's decision was a real disappointment. Before the 2002 Winter Olympics, a group called the United Icelandic Appeal launched a campaign. They called it "Falcons Forever."

They held a ceremony in Salt Lake City to raise awareness of the Falcons. Even Team Canada director Wayne Gretzky was there.

It was too late to change the uniforms in 2002, but suddenly the Winnipeg Falcons were big news again. Hockey fans everywhere were learning their story. Once again, people knew about the long-shot group of childhood friends who grew up to become Canada's first Olympic hockey champions.

In 2004, Team Canada wore uniforms just like the Falcons' golden yellow Olympic jerseys. In 2005, future National Hockey League stars like Sidney Crosby and Dion Phaneuf wore Falcons sweaters for Team Canada at the World Junior Championship.

It seems certain now that the story of the Winnipeg Falcons has a lasting place in hockey history.

Glossary

Assist: A pass that leads to a teammate scoring a goal

Application: A written request

Auditorium: An arena or big hall

Blocked shot: A shot of the puck stopped by a defending player before it reaches the goaltender or net

Combination play: A combination, or mix, of passes between two or more players

Body check: To stop an opponent from getting the puck by hitting him or her with the hips or shoulders

Deke: To briefly pretend to move in one direction in order to trick an opponent into going the wrong way

Disc: Another word for puck

Exhibition game: A game that is not part of the regular season

Faceoff: To drop the puck between two opposing centres to restart play after the game has been stopped

Intermediate league: The middle level of play between a junior league and a senior league

League: A collection of sports teams that compete against one another at different levels

Official: A person who makes sure the rules of the game are followed

Glossary

Offside: When a player enters the opposing team's zone ahead of the puck

Opponent: The challenging, or rival, player or team

Penalty: The punishment of a player for breaking rules by removing the player from the game for a period of time

Slashing: To hit an opponent with a hockey stick

Spectator: A person viewing the game

Stickhandling: To control the puck with a hockey stick by shifting it from one side of the blade to the other

Telegraph/telegram: A system of sending messages through wires before the telephone was invented

Acknowledgements

When people ask, I like to tell them it took me 15 days to write this book … but 15 years to do the research! That's a bit of an exaggeration, but not much.

I had just finished my first book (*Hockey Night in the Dominion of Canada*) back in 1992 when I decided that Frank Fredrickson's life story would make a great second novel. I never finished it, but the Canada Council Explorations Grant I received at that time helped launch my career. Now, it has resulted in this book.

When I began my research, there was no Internet as we know it today. All my early work involved trips to the library, making phone calls, writing letters, and travelling to different cities. It also involved a lot of photocopies. Fortunately, I kept those. Unfortunately, I have not done as well keeping track of the names of the

Acknowledgements

librarians and archivists in Toronto, Winnipeg, Ottawa, and London (both London, Ontario and London, England) who helped me along the way. Thank you to all of them. Thank you also to Stan Fischler, Ed Sweeney, Iain Fyffe, Frank Fredrickson and the late Marilyn Peppiat.

Nowadays, there are web sites that make research so much easier. I don't know how I could have written this book without the treasures on Brian Johannesson's Winnipeg Falcons site, nor the information on the Society for International Hockey Research site.

Still, it takes many people to turn research into a book. Among them, I want to thank Rebecca Sjonger for her insightful queries. A special thank you to Hadley Dyer, and to Lorimer, for helping me, finally, write this story.

About the Author

ERIC ZWEIG is a managing editor with Dan Diamond and Associates, consulting publishers to the NHL. He has written about sports and sports history for many major publications, including the *Toronto Star* and the *Globe and Mail*. He has also been a writer/producer with CBC Radio Sports and TSN SportsRadio, and written several popular books about hockey for both adults and children. He lives in Owen Sound, Ontario, with his family.

Photo Credits

The images in this book appear courtesy of Brian Johannesson. These images and more can be seen on his website: www.winnipegfalcons.com